297146

JM
ADL

WITHDRAWN

D0429193

*Donated
by*

THE RAPID CITY JOURNAL

1997

GRACE BALLOCH
MEMORIAL LIBRARY
625 North Fifth Street
Spearfish SD 57783-2311

A Houdini Club Magic Mystery

Lucky Stars

by David A. Adler

illustrated by Heather Harms Maione

GRACE BALLOCH
MEMORIAL LIBRARY
625 North Fifth Street
Spearfish SD 57783-2311

A FIRST STEPPING STONE BOOK

Random House 🏠 New York

For my nephew, Jacob Neumark

Text copyright © 1996 by David A. Adler
Illustrations copyright © 1996 by Heather Harms Maione
"The Lucky Stars Trick" copyright © 1996 by Bob Friedhoffer
All rights reserved under International and Pan-American Copyright
Conventions. Published in the United States by Random House, Inc.,
New York, and simultaneously in Canada by Random House of Canada
Limited, Toronto.

Library of Congress Cataloging-in-Publication Data
Adler, David A.
Lucky stars / by David A. Adler ; illustrated by Heather Harms Maione.
   p. cm. — (A Houdini Club magic mystery)
"A First stepping stone book."
SUMMARY: Herman "Houdini" Foster and his cousin Janet discover that
what seems to be a case of thwarted coat theft is something much more
serious.
ISBN 0-679-84698-0 (trade) — ISBN 0-679-94698-5 (lib. bdg.)
[1. Stealing—Fiction. 2. Magic tricks—Fiction. 3. Mystery and detective
stories.] I. Maione, Heather Harms, ill. II. Title. III. Series: Adler,
David A. Houdini Club magic mystery.
PZ7.A2615Lu 1996 [Fic]—dc20   94-33629

Manufactured in the United States of America   10 9 8 7 6 5 4 3 2 1

A HOUDINI CLUB MAGIC MYSTERY is a trademark of Random House, Inc.

★ Contents ★

J M
A D L

GRACE BALLOCH
MEMORIAL LIBRARY
625 North Fifth Street
Spearfish SD 57783-2311

A Houdini Club Magic Mystery

Lucky Stars

297146

1
Lucky Stars

"I AM THE GREAT HOUDINI!" my cousin said, real loud. "I CAN PREDICT THE FUTURE!"

My cousin Houdini Foster and I were on our way to the library. We were standing at the corner, waiting for the traffic light to change.

A man was waiting at the corner, too. When Houdini said he was great, the man looked at him.

I whispered, "You're embarrassing me. Someone is watching."

"Of course someone is watching," my cousin said. "Everyone wants to see the Great Houdini."

The traffic light changed. The man hurried across the street. He wanted to get away from us.

Houdini and I are in the same class at school. We were going to the library to work on our "My Hero" school projects. Ms. Kane, our teacher, told us to write a biography of someone we admire.

"Janet Perry, I can predict the future," Houdini said again. "And I'll prove it. I'll show you my Lucky Stars Trick."

Houdini's real name is Herman Foster.

But he doesn't like to be called Herman. He says it's too ordinary a name for someone so great.

Last year he read a book about Harry Houdini, who was once the world's greatest magician. Herman practiced magic and began calling *himself* Houdini. Now almost everyone calls him that.

We walked through the library parking lot.

"We don't have time for magic tricks," I told Houdini. "We have to work on our school projects. And we have to be at Dana's house by three o'clock."

Houdini said, "You worry too much about school. All you think about are tests and homework."

I turned to him. "School is important—Oops! Excuse me."

I was looking at Houdini. I wasn't watching where I was going. I bumped into a woman with long red hair.

"Excuse *me*," she said. She wasn't looking where she was going, either. She was watching a woman in a purple coat get out of her car.

When we reached the front steps of the library, Houdini stopped. He said real loud, "I PREDICT—MY LUCKY STARS TRICK WILL AMAZE YOU!"

An old man carrying lots of books was walking past us. I think he wanted to watch the Lucky Stars Trick, but the top book was about to drop. The man hurried to his car.

A teenager wearing lots of earrings was coming out of the library. He stopped to look at us.

Houdini was happy now. He had an audience.

"I'll watch your trick," I whispered. "But do it quietly."

Houdini reached into his backpack. He took out his magician's top hat and cape and put them on.

"Excuse me," the woman in the purple coat said as she walked up the steps.

"You're missing a great trick," Houdini told her.

"Excuse me," the red-haired woman said.

She was missing the trick, too.

A woman and two children walked down the steps. The children wanted to watch the trick, but the woman told them to hurry to the car.

Houdini reached into his coat pocket and pulled out a white envelope. Inside the envelope were three large paper stars. One star was yellow. One was blue. One was red.

He placed the stars on the library steps.

"Now pick one," he said.

"Aren't you going to predict the future?" I asked.

Houdini folded his arms and smiled. "I already did. This morning I wrote down which Lucky Star you will pick."

My favorite color is blue. Houdini knows that. This was my chance to trick him.

I pointed to the red star.

Houdini looked at me and said, "I knew you would pick red."

"Prove it!" I told him.

Houdini looked over at the teenager with lots of earrings. Then he smiled. It was one of his big magic show smiles.

"Janet, please turn over the red star," Houdini said.

I turned over the red star. There was a message written there. I read it aloud: "You will pick the red star."

"That's amazing!" the teenager said.

"Wait a minute," I said. "That's not so amazing. I'll bet there's a message on the backs of the blue and yellow stars, too."

Houdini was still smiling.

"Why don't you check?" he said.

I turned over the blue star. Then I turned over the yellow star.

The backs of those stars were blank.

★ 2 ★
How About That!

Houdini took off his hat and bowed.

"How did you know that I would pick the red star?" I asked.

Houdini smiled. It was another big magic show smile. I could see his back teeth.

He bowed again and said, "I am great. I can predict the future."

"No. Really. How did you know?"

Houdini waved to the teenager with the earrings.

Then he whispered to me, "It's a setup."

"What does that mean?" I asked.

"Sometimes a magician cheats a little," said Houdini. "He puts a deck of cards in a certain order. Or hides something up his sleeve. He sets up his trick beforehand so he knows it will work."

"How did you set up this trick?" I asked.

"I'll show you later, at our club meeting," Houdini said.

That's the Houdini Club. A few months ago Houdini started it. We meet in our friend Dana's basement. At the meetings Houdini does magic tricks. I think he started the club to show off how great a magician he is. But I don't mind. After he does a trick, he teaches us how to do it.

Houdini put the stars in the white envelope. He put the envelope in his pocket. He put the hat and cape in his backpack. Then we went into the library.

"Hello," I said to Amy.

Amy is the library guard, and she's real nice. Sometimes, after Houdini teaches me a trick, I show it to Amy. If I make a mistake, she pretends not to notice. When the trick is done, she acts real surprised and says, "How about that!"

Amy's job is to make sure no one steals books from the library.

I told Amy, "We're here to do research."

"You came to the right place," Amy said.

As we walked to the biography section,

I told Houdini, "I'm writing about Gertrude Ederle. She was the first woman to swim across the English Channel. People said a woman couldn't do it. But she did it. And she broke the men's speed record, too."

Houdini said, "Guess who I'm writing about."

"Don't tell me," I said. "I can predict the future, too. I predict that you will write about Harry Houdini."

"That's right," Houdini said.

It was obvious. We were working on a "My Hero" project. And Harry Houdini is my cousin's hero.

I found a book about women in sports. Gertrude Ederle was in the chapter on great swimmers.

Houdini found a book about Harry Houdini.

We went to the reference room. It has lots of places to sit and work. The room was crowded with people all busy reading and writing.

I found a side table with two empty seats.

We put our books on the table. Then we put our coats over the backs of our chairs and sat down.

Houdini started to read his book. He reads real fast. He's almost a genius.

"Listen to this," Houdini said. "In 1906 Harry Houdini did a great trick with three handkerchiefs. He borrowed the handkerchiefs from the audience."

"Sh!" the librarian said.

Houdini whispered, "He made the handkerchiefs disappear. He asked the audience where they wanted to find them. Someone called out, the Statue of Liberty. And they found one of the handkerchiefs there, in a sealed box."

I was tired of hearing about Harry Houdini. I wanted to do my work. I opened the book on women in sports.

I read for a while. Houdini was quiet. He was reading, too. He likes to read about the Great Harry Houdini.

"Hey, you're in my seat," someone said.

"Sh!" the librarian said again.

Houdini and I looked up. A tall woman with long black hair was standing by our table.

"I was sitting there," she said. "I went to

look for a book, and I left my coat over the
back of that chair. Hey! Where's my coat?
Who took my coat?"

★ 3 ★
The Missing Purple Coat

"I don't know where your coat is," I said. "I don't even know what it looks like."

"It's a beautiful coat," the woman said. "There's not another coat like it! It's long. It's a soft purple with red and orange flowers along the front. I sewed on the flowers myself."

Then I remembered.

"I did see your coat. I saw you wearing it when you walked past us on your way into the library. But I didn't take it," I said.

The woman looked real upset. She left our table and looked all around the reference room. She even looked under the tables. Then she came back to us.

"Someone stole my coat," she said.

"Don't worry," I told her. "My cousin is almost a genius. He'll find your coat."

Houdini said, "Whoever stole your coat probably took it out of the library."

"Let's ask Amy," I said. "Maybe she saw someone leave with it."

Before I left the reference room, I took my coat off the back of my chair and put it on.

"I'm not leaving it here," I said. "Someone might steal it."

Houdini put on his coat, too. We hadn't checked out our books yet, but we didn't want to forget them. We put them in our backpacks.

We walked to the library entrance. Amy was looking in someone's books to make sure they had all been checked out.

"Have you seen my coat?" the woman asked. "There's not another one like it. It's long, purple, and beautiful. I left it over a chair in the reference room, and now it's gone."

"Yes," Amy said. "I saw it when you came in. It's so purple. I said to myself, How about that coat!"

"Did anyone leave here with it?" the woman asked.

Amy shook her head. "No."

Houdini said, "Maybe someone stuffed the coat into a book bag and snuck out with it."

Amy shook her head again. "No. I check every bag."

A man was leaving the library. He was carrying a briefcase. He opened it so Amy could check inside.

Houdini said, "Maybe someone snuck out one of the other exits."

Amy shook her head and said, "The other exits are for emergencies only. If anyone opens one of those doors, an alarm goes off."

A woman with long red hair walked past.

Then a man walked past. He was carrying a big pile of books. Amy checked his books, and the man walked outside.

Houdini looked out the window. He

watched the man go down the front steps of the library and walk to his car.

"Look at all these windows," Houdini said.

There *were* a lot of windows.

"Maybe the thief opened one and threw the coat out," said Houdini. "Then he walked past you, went outside, and picked it up."

Amy smiled and shook her head for the fourth time. "It's winter. The windows are locked."

Houdini thought for a minute. I did, too. But I couldn't figure out how the thief got the purple coat out of the library.

"I know," Houdini said.

Amy shook her head.

Houdini said, "How do you know I'm wrong? You haven't even heard what I was going to say."

Amy said, "There's no way to get something big and purple out of this library without me seeing it."

Houdini smiled. "That's just what I was about to say. The purple coat could not have been taken out. *It must still be in the library.*"

★ 4 ★
I Don't Steal

Amy asked the woman, "Did you go to another part of the library? Maybe you took the coat with you and left it somewhere."

The woman thought for a moment. Then she said, "I did go to the new book section. I'll look there."

Houdini, Amy, and I watched the woman hurry off.

Then Amy told us, "She thinks her coat is beautiful. I think it's strange. Someone sewed spiders on the front."

"Those aren't spiders," I said. "They're flowers."

"Spiders. Flowers. Whatever," Amy said. "I don't think the coat was stolen. I think the woman misplaced it. People misplace things here all the time."

Houdini said, "I know a lot about people."

"You're almost a genius," I said.

"That's right. And that woman didn't misplace her coat. She loves it too much. Someone stole it. But I'll find it."

Houdini walked quickly down the main hall of the library.

I said good-bye to Amy and ran to catch up with him.

"If you stole a purple coat," Houdini asked me, "where would you put it?"

"I wouldn't steal a purple coat," I said. "I don't steal."

We went to the history section.

"Look," Houdini said. He pointed to a large bag on the floor. The bag was big enough to hide a coat. The man sitting next to it had lots of books. He was busy writing.

Houdini took out his pen. He walked past the man and dropped the pen right next to the bag. When he bent down to pick it up, he looked in the bag.

Houdini shook his head. He came back

to me and whispered, "It's full of news-
papers."

Houdini and I searched all through the
library. We looked under the desks and
tables. We even looked in the trash baskets.
But we didn't find the coat.

"We've looked everywhere," I said.

We started walking back to the library entrance. On the way we passed two closed doors. One had a sign that said WOMEN. The other was marked MEN.

"Wait! We didn't go in there," I said.

Houdini said, "I don't have to. I went at home, before we came to the library."

"I don't mean for *that*," I said. "Maybe the thief is in there with the coat. Or maybe that's where he hid it."

"Oh," Houdini said.

Houdini is almost a genius. But sometimes I'm the smart one.

★ 5 ★
I'm Coming In

"You check the women's room. I'll check the men's," Houdini said.

I went into the women's room.

There are three sinks, three mirrors, and three stalls in the bathroom.

First I checked by the sinks and mirrors. No coat.

Then I went into the first stall. Whoever was there before me didn't flush.

Yuck!

I pushed the flush stick down with my foot. Then I looked on the hook behind the door.

No coat.

I went to the next stall.

No coat.

The door to the last stall was closed. But I didn't hear anyone in there.

I pushed on the door. It was locked. If someone was in there, she was being very quiet.

I knocked.

"Hello?" I said.

No one answered.

"If you're in there, please say something."

There was still no answer.

I bent down and looked under the door. I didn't see any feet.

In a movie I once saw, someone went into a bathroom to hide from the police. He stood on the toilet so when the police looked under the door they wouldn't see his feet. In the movie it was a man. But a woman could do that, too.

"If you don't say anything, I'm coming in."

No one said anything.

The floor was dirty. I didn't want to crawl under the door. But I had to. I had to find out if the purple coat was in there.

I got down on my knees. I put my backpack on the floor next to me. Then I bent my head and crawled.

The police should have done this in the movie. They would have caught their man at the beginning of the movie instead of at the end.

As I crawled under the door, I looked.
There was no one in the stall. When I was
all the way in, I turned around.

And there it was.

★ 6 ★
Not Again

The purple coat was hanging on the hook on the back of the door.

Amy was right. The flowers *did* look like spiders.

I took the coat off the hook. Then I unlocked the door and left the stall. I picked up my backpack and walked out of the bathroom.

Houdini was outside waiting for me.

"Here's the coat," I said. "I found it hanging in there."

Houdini took it from me and said, "It sure is an ugly coat. Let's find the woman and give it back."

The woman was at the entrance with Amy. She was filling out a Lost Property report. When she saw us with the coat, she got all excited.

"That's it! That's my coat!" she said.

Amy said, "How about that!"

"Thank you. Oh, thank you so much!" the woman said to Houdini as she put on the coat.

"Isn't it beautiful?" she asked.

I didn't want to lie, so I didn't say anything.

"We found it in the bathroom," Houdini said.

We!

"I didn't see you in the women's bathroom with me. Were you there?" I asked Houdini. "Do you often go into the women's bathroom?"

When I said that, a woman with long red hair turned to look. And a man in a green shirt laughed real loud.

Houdini gave me an angry look. I gave him one right back.

"You see. I was right," Amy told the woman with the purple coat. "You misplaced it."

"I didn't misplace my coat," the woman said. "I don't misplace things. I never even went to the bathroom."

The woman said, "I still have work to do. But I'll do it with my coat on. I don't want to lose this again."

After the woman walked away, I said, "The coat was hanging in one of the stalls. No one was in there and the door was locked. I had to crawl under the door. The thief went to a lot of trouble to keep us from finding that coat."

Houdini asked, "Why would he steal a coat and then leave it there?"

"She," I said. "The thief is a woman. I know that because she left the coat in the women's bathroom."

"The thief must have realized she couldn't get the coat past me," Amy said. "You know, we have real good security in this library."

"The important thing," I said, "is that we found the coat. Now we can get back to our schoolwork."

I opened my backpack and took out the women in sports book.

"Excuse me," a short man with white hair said to Amy. "My coat is missing. It's brown and has a fur collar. I left it on the back of my chair. Then I went to look for a book. Now it's gone."

"Oh, no!" I said. "Not again!"

★ 7 ★
He's Thinking

"Don't worry," Houdini told the man. "We already found one coat today. We'll find yours, too."

He said *we* again!

"*I* found the first coat in the women's bathroom," I said. I made sure to say the *I* part real loud. "Maybe *I* should check there again."

Amy said, "That's a good idea."

I put the sports book in my backpack again.

I went back into the bathroom. A woman was standing by the sinks. She had long brown hair. She was brushing it and looking in the mirror.

She put a barrette in her hair and asked me, "Do you like my hair this way?"

Then she took out the barrette and tied a bow around her hair. Now it was in a ponytail. "Or do you like it this way better?"

"I like it better with a ponytail," I said. "It's neater."

I walked past the woman to the three stalls. This time the door on the third stall was open. But the door on the first stall was closed.

I pushed the door to the first stall. It was locked. I knocked and asked, "Is anyone in there?"

No one answered.

"Try another one. They're open," the woman standing by the sinks told me.

I knocked again. "If you're in there, speak up," I said.

"Use another one," the woman said.

I turned and looked at her. She looked silly. She had three pigtails. There was a small one on the top of her head, and two bigger ones in the back.

I got down on my knees. I didn't see any feet. I put my backpack on the floor. Then I bent my head and crawled under the stall door.

Once I was inside the stall, I turned around. I saw a brown coat with a fur collar hanging on the hook.

I took the coat off the hook and unlocked the door.

The woman by the sinks was staring at me.

I wanted to tell the woman that I had just found a stolen coat, and that I was helping solve a mystery. But I was in a hurry.

"Someone I know left it here," I said. "I'm giving it back to him."

"Him!" she said. "How did *he* leave *his* coat in the women's bathroom?"

I didn't answer. I just smiled and picked up my backpack.

I told the woman, "I think you looked better with the ponytail."

Then I left the bathroom.

The short man with white hair was waiting with Amy and Houdini. He was

real happy when I gave him his coat.

"I'm so glad you found it!" he said. "It's not an expensive coat. The fur on the collar is fake. But it keeps me warm."

"Well, that's it," I said. "The mysteries

are solved. Both coats have been found. Now we can do our school projects."

"Not yet," Houdini said. "We still don't know who stole the coats and why."

"The thief must not be too smart," I said to Amy. "If she couldn't get out with one coat, why did she take another one?"

"I don't know," said Amy.

"Is he all right?" the man asked. He was looking at Houdini.

Houdini's eyes were closed. He was rubbing his forehead.

"He's thinking," I said.

I looked at my watch. It was two-thirty. The Houdini Club meeting was in just half an hour.

"You'd better think fast," I told Houdini.

Amy said to me, "While we're waiting, why don't you show us a trick?"

"Okay," I said. "I'm learning a new one. It's a prediction trick. I'll give you three stars. I'll ask you to pick one, and I'll predict which one you'll pick."

"How about that!" Amy said.

"Houdini," I said. "Can I use your Lucky Stars?"

He didn't answer. He was still thinking.

I reached into Houdini's coat pocket and took out the white envelope.

Houdini opened his eyes. He looked at me and then at the envelope.

"I'm just borrowing your Lucky Stars," I said.

Houdini stared at his empty pocket.

Then he closed his eyes and rubbed his forehead again.

I took the three Lucky Stars out of the envelope. I made sure Amy couldn't see the message on the back of the red star. Then I put the stars on her desk.

I told Amy, "Pick one."

Houdini is real smart. He's almost a genius. He told me he set up the trick, so I was sure it would work. I was sure Amy would pick the red star.

Amy looked at the stars. She looked at me. Then she pointed to the blue star.

I was wrong.

Houdini was wrong.

The trick didn't work!

I was just about to tell Amy when

Houdini yelled, "I've got it! When you reached into my pocket, you helped me solve the mystery!"

"I did?"

"This mystery is like my Lucky Stars Trick," said Houdini. "It's a setup! When the thief stole the coats, she already knew what was in the pockets."

I didn't get it.

"Wait right here," Houdini said. Then he ran off.

I hate it when he does that.

8

Call the Police!

In a few minutes Houdini came running back with the woman in the purple coat.

Houdini told her, "There's something missing from your pockets."

Then he told the man, "There's something missing from your pockets, too."

The man reached into his pants pockets.

"I don't think anything is missing," he

said. "My wallet is here." He opened it. "And my money is here, too."

"There wouldn't be anything missing from your *pants* pockets," I told the man. "The thief took your coat, not your pants."

The man took a comb and two pens from his coat pockets.

Meanwhile, the woman in the purple coat searched in her coat pockets. Then she searched through her handbag.

"My car keys are gone," she said.

The man searched again through his coat pockets. "My car keys are gone, too!" he said.

Houdini said, "I knew it. The thief took your coats to get your keys. She took your keys so she could steal your cars."

"Oh, my!" the woman said. The man didn't say anything.

They both ran to the door. Houdini and I followed them.

"Wait!" Amy called out to us. "You can't leave. I have to check your backpacks. It's my job!"

We waited while Amy looked through Houdini's backpack. She found the Harry Houdini book.

Amy told Houdini, "This book has to be checked out before you can leave the library."

She looked at my book and told me the same thing.

The woman in the purple coat came back inside.

"My car is still in the lot," she told us. "It takes more than keys to steal it. You need to know my secret code, 2-4-5-1."

Her secret code wasn't a secret anymore.

Then the man came into the library.

"It's gone," he said. "My car is gone. And everything I had in the car is gone, too."

I just stood there. I didn't know what to say.

"Tomorrow is my granddaughter's birthday," the man said. "She likes to play chess, so I bought her a fancy chess set. It was on the back seat of my car."

"I'll call the police," said Amy.

"Tell them to look for an old red car," said the man.

Houdini said, "And tell them that a woman with long red hair is driving it."

How did he know that?

★ 9 ★
Houdini Explains

Houdini told the woman in the purple coat, "I saw you getting out of your car this morning. A woman with long red hair was watching you."

"That's right!" I said. "I remember her, too."

"Then I did a trick on the steps of the library," Houdini said to the woman. "You walked right past. And the woman with red hair was behind you."

That's why Houdini remembered them. They didn't watch his trick.

Houdini said, "It was a setup. The woman with the red hair watched you put your keys in your coat pocket. Then she followed you inside the library. When you took your coat off, she stole it. She took out the keys and hid the coat in the bathroom."

Houdini looked at Amy.

"Then the thief went outside to steal the car. It was easy for her to get past you because she wasn't carrying any books. Just some keys."

"How about that!" Amy said.

"But the thief couldn't steal my car," the woman said. "She didn't know my secret code."

"So she started all over again!" I said. "I get it!"

I looked at the man with the brown coat.

"The thief watched you put your keys in your coat pocket, too," I told him. "She stole your coat and your keys. Then she went outside to steal your car."

"And I don't have a secret code," the man said sadly.

Just then we saw the police. They came in two cars. The first was a police car. The light on the top was flashing. Behind it was an old red car.

The cars stopped. A police officer got out of the red car and came into the library.

"That red car is mine!" the man told the police officer.

"Where are my keys?" the woman in the purple coat asked.

"The thief was the woman with red hair, wasn't she?" Houdini asked.

The officer nodded.

"I solved the mystery," said Houdini. "I should get a reward. I'd like a police badge or a medal. And I think the mayor should give it to me at a big ceremony."

The officer looked at Amy and said, "Help!"

"I need my keys," the woman said. "I can't get into my car without them."

"And I want my car back," the man said.

"Wait! Stop! Quiet!" the officer said. "You'll get everything back. But it will take a little time."

TIME!

★ 10 ★
I Am the Great Houdini

I looked at my watch.

"We're late," I told Houdini. "We're late again for our Houdini Club meeting."

I checked out my women in sports book. Houdini checked out his Houdini book.

When we showed our books to Amy, she said, "You never told me. Did you predict that I would pick the blue star?"

I shook my head and said, "I thought you would pick the red one."

"How about that!" Amy said. "At first, I was going to pick the red star. And you knew it. How about that!"

Amy is real nice.

Houdini and I left the library. We walked carefully through the parking lot. A parking lot is like a street, you know.

When we got to Dana's house, she was on her front porch, waiting for us.

"You're late," she said. "You're always late."

"I'm worth waiting for," Houdini told her. "I have a great trick to teach you."

Dana and I followed Houdini to the basement. There was a table and chairs set up. Everyone from the Houdini Club was there. Jordan, Melissa, Rachel, Daniel, Maria, and Tony.

Houdini went into the laundry room to prepare his trick. While he was in there, I told everyone what happened at the library.

"I can't believe you caught a car thief!" Rachel said.

Houdini came into the room. He had on his top hat and cape. He was carrying the white envelope.

"I AM THE GREAT HOUDINI," he said real loud. "I CAN PREDICT THE FUTURE. I PREDICT—MY LUCKY STARS TRICK WILL AMAZE YOU."

Houdini took the three stars from the

envelope and placed them on the table. He told Melissa to pick one.

She pointed to the yellow star.

Aha! I said to myself. Melissa didn't pick the red star. Houdini's magic didn't work!

But Houdini smiled. He said, "Melissa, please take off my hat and look inside."

Melissa took Houdini's hat off his head.

"There's a message here!" she said. "It says: You will pick the yellow star."

Suddenly I knew how Houdini did the trick. It was so easy!

Now I knew what he meant when he said the trick was a setup.

"What a great trick!" Tony said.

"How did you do it?" Rachel asked.

"I, the Great Houdini, will teach you," said Houdini.

Houdini told them how to do the Lucky Stars Trick. But I didn't listen.

Instead, I took the women in sports book from my backpack. Finally I could do some schoolwork.

★ The Lucky Stars Trick ★
★ ★ by Bob Friedhoffer ★ ★

EFFECT:

The magician predicts which of three paper stars a volunteer will pick.

PROPS: A table

Three pieces of construction
paper—one blue, one yellow,
and one red

An envelope

Scissors

Clear tape

A black pen

PREPARATION:

• Cut a star, about 3" across, from each piece of construction paper.

• Cut a square, about 1" x 2", from the

blue and the yellow pieces of construction paper.

- On the blue square, write: YOU WILL PICK THE BLUE STAR. On the yellow square, write: YOU WILL PICK THE YELLOW STAR. On the red *star*, write: YOU WILL PICK THE RED STAR.

- Put the blue square into the envelope and tuck it into one corner. Tape the yellow square underneath the table. Put the three colored stars into the envelope. Make sure that the message on the red star is facedown.

ROUTINE AND PATTER:

"I can predict the future! And I'll prove it with the help of my Lucky Stars."

- Pick a volunteer from the audience.

- Take the three colored stars out of the

envelope and lay them on the table in front of the volunteer. Be careful not to let anyone see the message on the red star. The blue square should stay hidden inside the envelope.

"Please pick one of the Lucky Stars. Then I'll show you that I knew exactly which star you would pick."

• If the volunteer picks the blue star, tell him or her to look inside the envelope. If the volunteer picks the yellow star, tell him or her to look underneath the table. If the red star is chosen, tell the volunteer to turn the red star over.

"Please read the message out loud."

• Everyone will be surprised that you "predicted" which star the volunteer would choose!

• NOTE: You can have a lot of fun with this trick. You can hide the blue and yellow squares in all sorts of places—under your hat, in your shoe, in someone else's pocket. But you should *never* repeat this trick for anyone. If they see it more than once, they will know that there is more than one message written down.

How do you change an onion into chocolate syrup?
Find out in...
Onion Sundaes

"My cousin says she doesn't like onions," Houdini said. "I guess I'll have to change this onion into something she does like."

Houdini dropped the onion into the top of the red paper tube.

He waved his magic wand and said, "*Ala-kazam,* I am great. Yes, I am."

Then he picked up the tube.

There on the table was a jar of chocolate syrup!

"How did you do that?" I asked.

From *Onion Sundaes*
(A Houdini Club Magic Mystery book)
by David A. Adler

How do you make a playing card disappear?
Find out in...
Wacky Jacks

"Now put the Wacky Jack back on the deck," said Houdini.

Mr. Fish put the card on top of the deck.

Houdini took out his magic wand. He waved it over the cards. "*Ala-kazam,* I am great. Yes, I am," he said.

Houdini tapped the deck with the wand and gave it to Mr. Fish. "Now see if you can find the Wacky Jack."

Mr. Fish turned the cards over.

The Wacky Jack was gone.

From *Wacky Jacks*
(A Houdini Club Magic Mystery book)
by David A. Adler

GRACE BALLOCH
MEMORIAL LIBRARY
625 North Fifth Street
Spearfish SD 57783-2311

297146

About the Authors

DAVID A. ADLER was one of six children in his family. "I used to do magic tricks to get attention," he says. "Now I write books to get attention!"

David has written many books for kids, including the acclaimed *Cam Jansen* series. He lives in New York with his wife and their three sons.

BOB FRIEDHOFFER, known as the "Madman of Magic," created the Lucky Stars Trick. Bob has been a magician for over fifteen years, and has even performed at the White House. He currently lives and works in New York City.